Gulp! It's the NUMBERS burp.
Count you in?

Robot Burp Smarty

For the loud ones

First edition 2014

Library of Congress Catalog Card Number 2013943079
ISBN 978-0-7636-6582-1

TLF 18 17 16 15 14 13
10 9 8 7 6 5 4 3 2 1

Printed in Dongguan, Guangdong, China

This book was typeset in Officina Sans.
The illustrations were created digitally in QuarkXPress.

Candlewick Press
99 Dover Street
Somerville, Massachusetts 02144

visit us at www.candlewick.com

Head,

pants!

Annette Simon

CANDLEWICK PRESS

Mmm-mmm, motor oil.
Nutty and bolty and tinny and—

brrp!

Oops! Please excuse me.
A screw must be loose.

Affirma —**brrp!**— irmative.
Oops! Please excuse ME!

Certain —**brrp!**— ertainly.

Tee-hee! Oops, again.
I beg your pardon.

Of — **brrp!** — course!
Tee-hee-hee!
I beg YOUR pardon.

ga-lug
ga-lugg

guzzle
guzz

2-3—rrp!

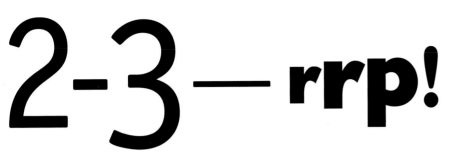

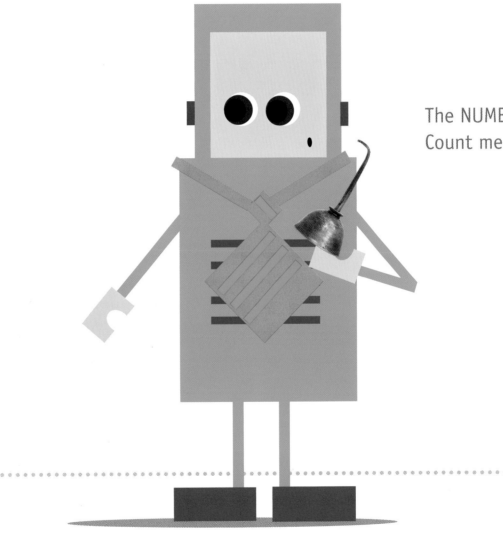

The NUMBERS burp!
Count me in!

Brrr—1-2-3-4-

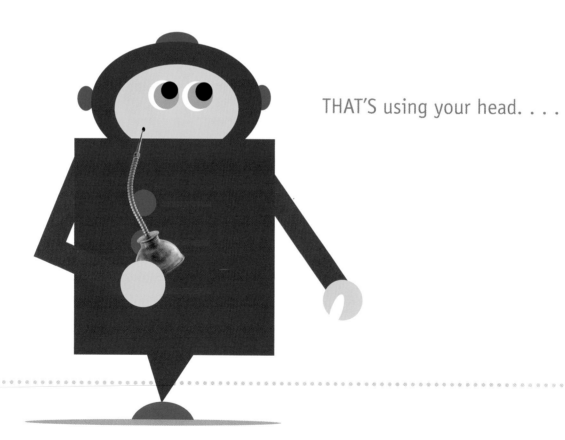

THAT'S using your head. . . .

Brrr—1-2-3-4-5-6-7-8-9-

10 — **rrp!**

The wheels are
turning now. . . .

Brrr—1-2-3-4-5-6-7-8-9-10-20-30

What a MACHINE!
Time to switch gears. . . .

Brrr —1-2-3-4-5-6-7-8-9-10-20-30

40-50-A-B-C-D—rrp!

I know what comes next. . . .

Brrr—

1-2-3-4-5-6-7-8-9-10-20-30-40-50-

A-B-C-D-E-I-E-I-O

With-a-zoink-zoink-here-and-

here-a-ZOINK-THERE-A-ZOINK

Old-MacDonald-had-a-

a-zoink-zoink-there-

-EVERYWHERE-a-zoink-zoink!

farm-E-I-E-I-rrrp!

ga-lug
ga-lugg

Hmm, no more oil.

No more nutty
or bolty
or tinny
or —

guzzle
guzz

Sounded like a
loose screw.

Her database
needs work,
but her speakers?
A-1!

Next time,
the REAL alphabelch.
No zoinks.

You're on.

Once I find some of those speakers. . . .

brrp!

A B C D E F G
M N O
U V W

You're on!
The REAL alphabelch.
No zoinks!